I AM THE DOG

By Daniel Pinkwater
Illustrated by Jack E. Davis

HARPER
An Imprint of HarperCollinsPublishers

One night we decided to change places.
"What do you say, Max? Tomorrow you can be me,
and I will be you."
Max liked the idea.
Max slept in my bed. I slept on the rug.

When we woke up in the morning, Max was the boy and I was the dog.
I stretched. I yawned. I scratched behind my ear—
all things I had seen Max do.
I could tell already I was going to like being a dog.

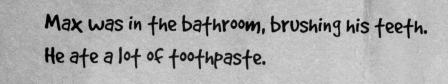

Max was in the bathroom, brushing his teeth.
He ate a lot of toothpaste.

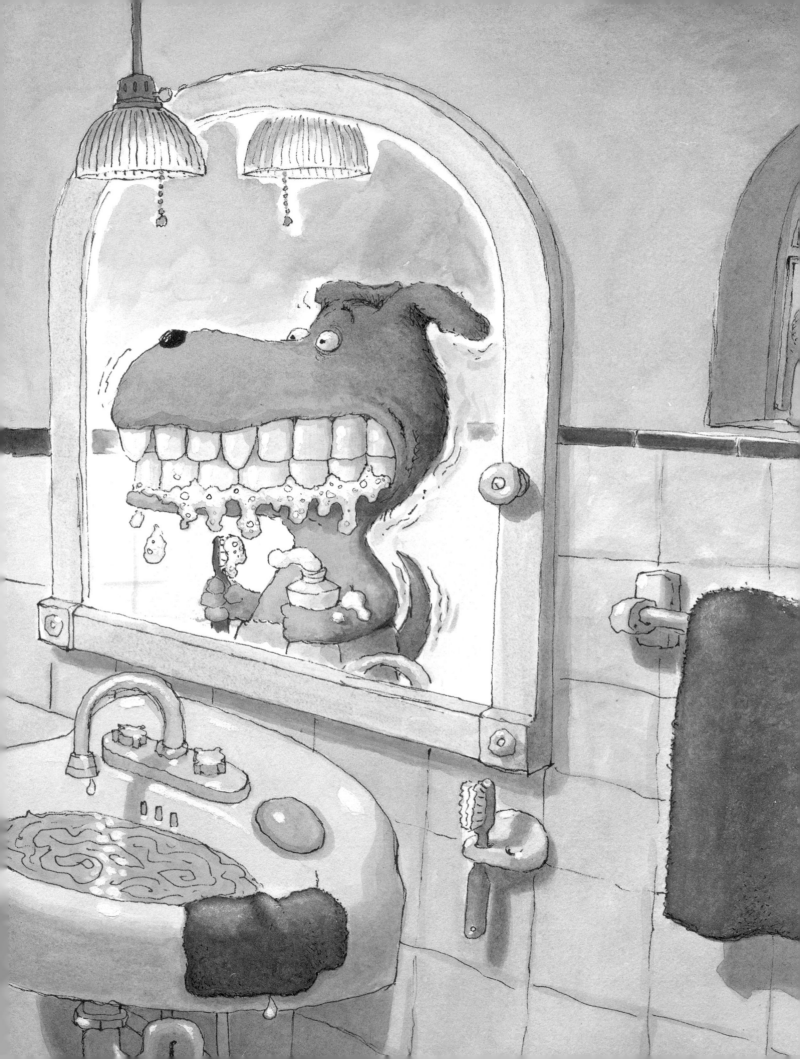

We went downstairs. The family was having breakfast.
"Have some cereal, dear," my mother said.
"I am the dog today," I said. "Could you put
my bowl on the floor?"
"Certainly, dear. Would you like your
orange juice in a bowl too?"
Max sat at the table and ate
with the family. He liked that.

"May I run around in the yard now?" I asked my mother.

"Yes," my mother said. "But stay away from my bushes!"

My mother drove Max to school.
The kids were all happy to see Max.
They all wanted to pet him and feed him things.
I could see that Max liked being in school.

After school Max took
me to the park.
The park is great when
you're a dog.
There are so many
things to sniff.

There are so
many trees.

I chased a squirrel.

I met another dog.

A lady gave me a cookie.

Max threw a ball.

I ran after it.

He threw it again.

For some reason, I never get tired of doing that.

He threw it again.

I ran after it again.

I ran after it again.

When Max got tired of throwing the ball, he scratched my ears. I liked that too.

At home I got in trouble.
I ate my Max's homework.

"The dog ate my homework!" Max said.
"My teacher will never believe this!"
My mother made me stay in the garage for an hour.
Max got to play video games.

My father came home. I was happy to see him.
I jumped up. I kissed his face.
"Look, Jacob! You get kibble
for supper!"

I love kibble! I love kibble! I love kibble. I could eat kibble every day for the rest of my life! I don't even know what kibble is. But I love kibble! Max had spaghetti and meatballs. He liked it.

THE DOG

After supper I felt like running around in the yard again.

In the evening the family was together in the living room.
My father sat in his armchair. He watched TV.
My mother read a book.

Max had to do his homework over again.
I snoozed.

I was happy.

That night I slept in my bed, and Max slept on his rug.
When we woke up in the morning, Max was the dog again,
and I was the boy. That's how things are supposed to be.
But both of us had learned something.

Being a dog is better.

To Lulu and Maxine
—Daniel Pinkwater

For Duggan, Sarge, Cindy, Honey, Mrs. Nichols, Reilly, Spike, Larry, Finnigan,
Nipper, Lucy, Baby, Luke, and Pudge. Loving friends and terrific dogs all.
—Jack E. Davis

I Am the Dog
Text copyright © 2010 by Daniel Pinkwater
Illustrations copyright © 2010 by Jack E. Davis

Printed in the United States of America.
Library of Congress Cataloging-in-Publication Data is available.
ISBN 978-0-06-055505-4 (trade bdg.)   ISBN 978-0-06-055506-1 (lib. bdg.)

Designed by Stephanie Bart-Horvath
10 11 12 13   LPR   10 9 8 7 6 5 4 3
❖
First Edition